The Adventures of
TOBALÍ

written by Florencia Alecha
illustrated by Agustina Barriola

isla
Tobalia

Tobalí

Mar Andaman

Tobali is 9 years old, and was chosen by
her tribe to be the queen of Tobalia.

Tobalia is a giant island on the inside and a miniature island
on the outside. Tobalia is so small that it can hardly be seen,
that is why no one knows where it is.

Many believe that it is one of the little dots that appear on the
maps when you look at the Andaman Sea. Others say that it
doesn't exist and that all of Tobalia is just a story.

On the Island of Tobalia, Tobali has the power to create everything she imagines. When she was very little, she invented a friend whom she called Patoleón.

Patoleón is half duck and half lion. He has the grace of a duck and the bravery of a lion and he is very intelligent!

Tobali is fun, super creative, and very restless. She can't sit still for a second. Even in her sleep she does amazing things! What she dreams about in her sleep comes true when she wakes up.

One day Tobali dreamed of a sky with rainbows, stars, and rabbits with ties. When she woke up...there they were! Two thousand jumping rabbits with ties filled the colorful sky.

The rabbits made her laugh so much
that her belly hurt for a week.

Tobali remembered that she could change
that too—just by using her imagination!

Tobali changed her belly pain into butterflies!

The butterflies flew her so far away that
she didn't know how to get back home.

It was getting very dark and Tobali doesn't like the dark night so she quickly tried to imagine something to get her back home. Tobali was so scared that she couldn't come up with any ideas.

Tobali, unable to imagine a way home,
thought of her friend Patoleón.

Patoleón immediately appeared in the clouds,
put her on his back and took her back to Tobalia.

Happy to be back home, Tobali had warm soup, put on her favorite pajamas, and got into bed to have another amazing dream...

To Mía, Francesca, Felicitas and Catalina, heirs of an invisible empire
-but no less strong for that-

F.A.

No part of this publication may be reproduced in whole or in part, stored in a retrieval system, or transmitted in any form or by any means, electronic, mechanical, photocopying, recording, or otherwise, without prior written permission of the publisher. For information regarding permission, write to the publisher, Storybook Genius, at: 220 Jefferson Street, Washington, Missouri 63090 or visit them at sbgpublishing.com ISBN 978-1-952954-77-1

CPSIA information can be obtained
at www.ICGtesting.com
Printed in the USA
BVRC101118190522
637506BV00003B/16